Star Light, Star Bright

Exploring Our Solar System

RED CHAIR PRESS

by

Anna Prokos

illustrated by

Dave Clegg

Imagine That! books are produced
and published by Red Chair Press
Red Chair Press LLC   PO Box 333
South Egremont, MA 01258-0333
www.redchairpress.com

 FREE Lesson Plans from Lerner eSource
and at www.redchairpress.com

Publisher's Cataloging-In-Publication Data
(Prepared by The Donohue Group, Inc.)

Names: Prokos, Anna. | Clegg, Dave, illustrator.
Title: Star light, star bright : exploring our solar system /
by Anna Prokos ; illustrated by Dave Clegg.

Description: South Egremont, MA : Red Chair Press, [2017] | Imagine
   that! | Interest age level: 006-009. | Includes Fact File data, a glossary
   and references for additional reading. | Includes bibliographical
   references and index. | Summary: "Have you ever laid on the ground
   at night looking up at the twinkling stars? Those stars are the millions
   of planets, moons, suns and space dust that make up the Milky Way
   Galaxy. Our Solar System lives in this galaxy and we are viewing
   Earth's neighbors when we look at the night sky. Sometimes you
   might see a shooting star streak across the sky. This is usually a
   meteoroid, small rock or ice that enters the Earth's atmosphere and
   burns up. Imagine what it must be like to zip through space and look
   back to Earth where kids around the globe are gazing into the night
   sky. Includes the most up-to-date findings from the New Horizons
   satellite."-- Provided by publisher.

Identifiers: LCCN 2016934112 | ISBN 978-1-63440-152-4 (library
   hardcover) | ISBN 978-1-63440-158-6 (paperback) | ISBN 978-1-63440-
   164-7 (ebook)

Subjects: LCSH: Solar system--Juvenile literature. | Stars--Juvenile
   literature. | Earth (Planet)--Juvenile literature. CYAC: Solar system.
   | Stars. | Earth (Planet).

Classification: LCC QB501.3 .P76 2017 (print) | LCC QB501.3 (ebook)
   | DDC 523.2--dc23

Technical charts by Joe LeMonnier
Photo credits: Shutterstock, Inc

First Edition by:
Red Chair Press LLC   PO Box 333   South Egremont,
MA 01258-0333

Printed in the United States of America
Distributed in the U.S. by Lerner Publisher Services.
www.lernerbooks.com

1116 1P CGBS17

Have you ever laid on the ground at night looking up at the twinkling stars? Those stars are the millions of **planets**, moons, suns and space dust that make up the Milky Way **galaxy**.

Our solar system lives in this galaxy and we are viewing Earth's neighbors when we look at the night sky. Sometimes you might see a shooting star streak across the sky. This is usually a meteoroid — small rock or ice that enters the Earth's **atmosphere** and burns up. Imagine what it must be like to zip through space and look back to Earth where kids around the globe are gazing into the night sky.

Table of Contents

It was a perfect summer night for a camp-out. Jackson was star-gazing with his best friend, Wyatt.

"Look, a shooting star!" Jackson said, pointing to the sky. A shiny streak raced above them.

"Quick!" Wyatt exclaimed. "Make a wish upon a star!"

The two friends squeezed their eyes tight.
They wished their wildest wishes.

Max knew exactly what to wish for, too.

When Jackson and Wyatt opened their eyes, they had a big surprise!

"Where on Earth are we?" Wyatt wondered.
"We're in space!" Jackson exclaimed.

"But...how did we get here?"
"Anything's possible when you wish upon a star!"
Wyatt reminded his buddy.

"The sun is a star, so make another wish!" Jackson said.

"I wish we could go planet-hopping!" Wyatt said.

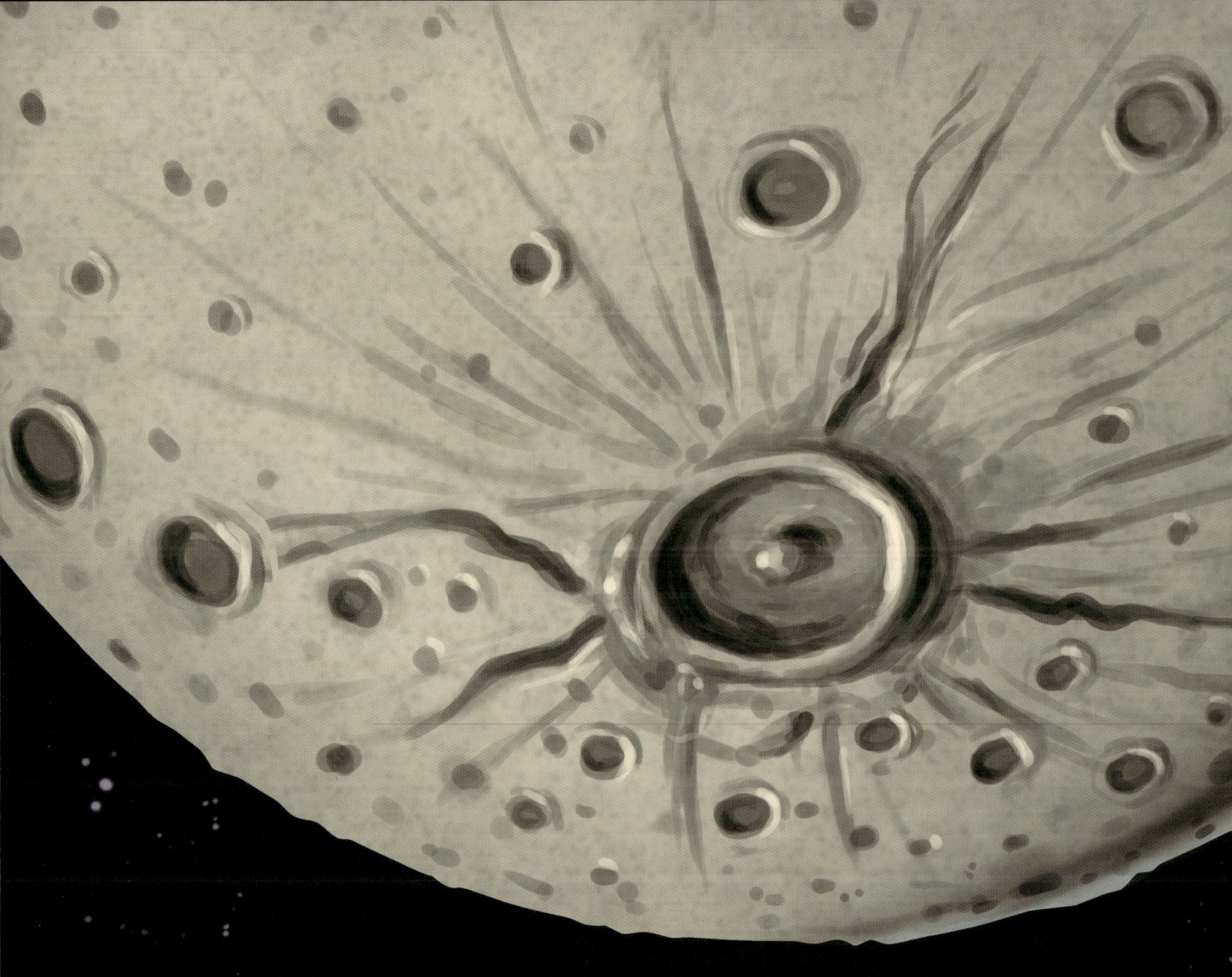

Suddenly, their ship sped through space. It almost collided with a planet! "That's Mercury, the planet closest to the sun," Jackson said. "It's the first stop on our planet hop!"

The friends stared at the rocky, gray surface. Steep, sharp cliffs rose up from the ground. They saw deep craters and dark ditches.

"Let's ditch Mercury," Jackson said. "Next stop: Venus!"

Wyatt steered ahead. "How do you know where to go next?" he asked Jackson.

"Just remember this: My Very Excellent Mother Just Served Us Noodles!" Jackson told Wyatt.

"Noodles?" Wyatt was confused. "What do noodles have to do with planets?"

IT'S A FACT

Venus is the hottest planet. The temperature reaches 800 to 900 degrees Fahrenheit — nearly twice as hot as a fire on Earth!

Jackson chuckled. "It's a trick to help you remember the order of the known planets. The first letter of every word begins with the first letter of a planet."

"Don't fly too close to Venus!" warned Jackson. "The thick clouds trap the sun's heat."

The space shuttle raced towards Earth.
"Home sweet home!" Jackson cheered.

Max howled at a glowing sphere near Earth.
"Max only howls at the moon," Wyatt said.
"So that must be it!"

As the boys got closer to the moon, they noticed lots of ditches and canyons on the powdery surface.

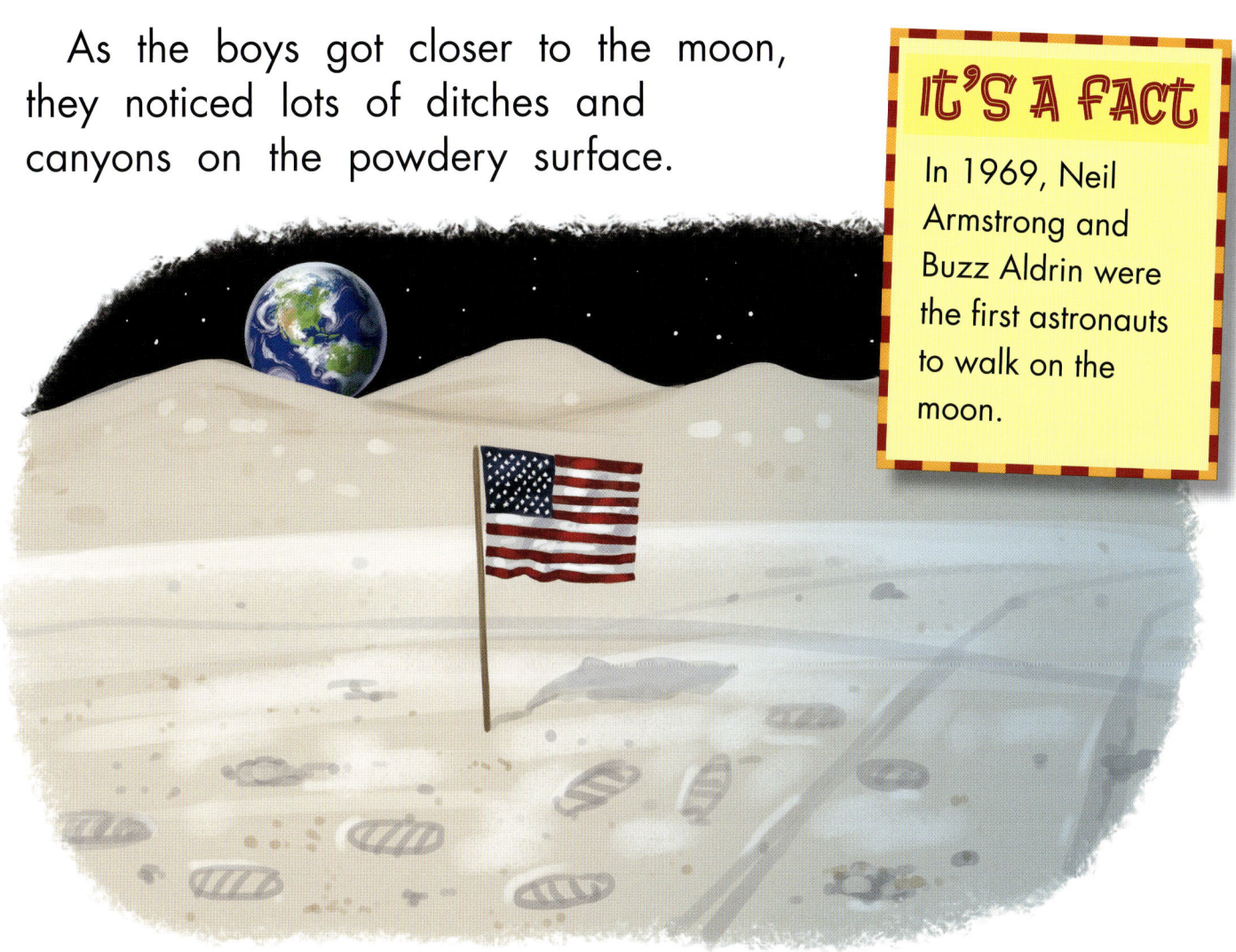

"Millions of years ago, meteors crashed into the moon and left their mark," Jackson explained. "There's no air or weather on the moon, so nothing ever changes here."

"You can still see the footprints of the first astronauts on the moon!" Wyatt added.

"So based on our planet sentence, an M planet must be next."

The ship blasted through space for 140 million miles. Suddenly, a cinnamon-colored globe loomed ahead.

"Mars!" Wyatt shouted. "The fourth planet from the sun."

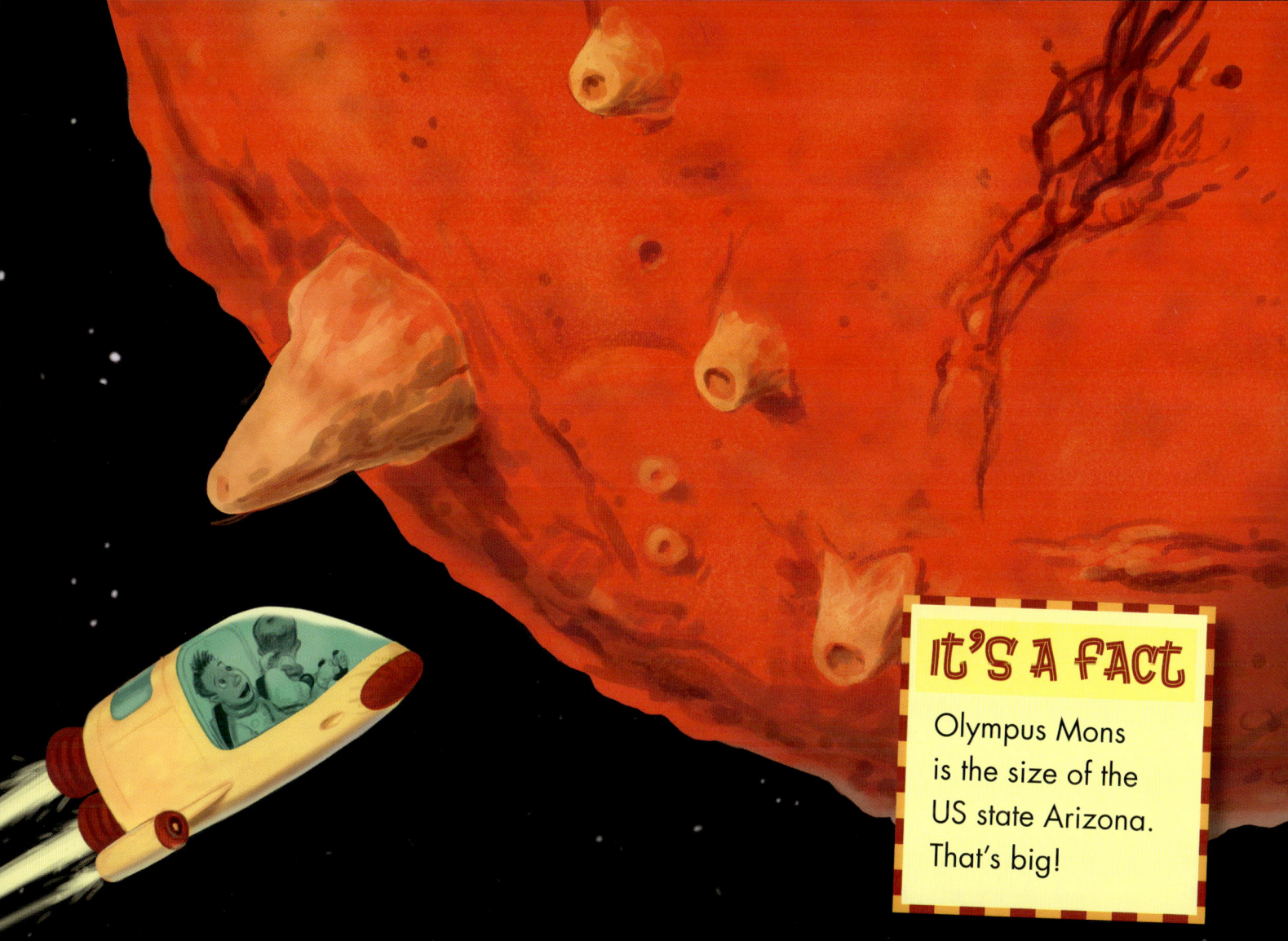

Rust-colored dirt and rocks covered Mars' surface. The boys noticed a giant mountain bigger than anything they had ever seen on Earth. It was Olympus Mons, the largest volcano in the solar system.

"Let's get out of here before it blows its top!" Wyatt urged.

Next, the spaceship sped off towards Jupiter. A jumble of moons surrounded the fast-spinning giant. Wyatt and Jackson couldn't believe the planet's size!

They saw a huge red storm cloud swirl across the planet. "That's the Great Red Spot," Jackson said. "It's a storm that has lasted for about 300 years."

IT'S A FACT

Jupiter is so big, about 1,300 Earths could fit inside it.

"Good thing Earth storms don't last that long,"
Wyatt joked. "Now let's get to our next stop!"

Out the window, the boys saw total darkness. Jackson checked the odometer. It read 890,700,000 miles! That's how far away they were from the sun. No wonder it was so dark!

"That is one cool planet!" Wyatt exclaimed, as he pointed to Saturn. He was right. Saturn's temperature is 320 degrees Fahrenheit below freezing. Saturn's rings are like giant ice blizzards,

"Let's land here," Wyatt said as he steered towards the rings.

"No way!" Jackson warned. "Saturn doesn't have a solid surface. If we tried to land, we would be sucked into the planet's core. Let's just blast on to Uranus!"

23

IT'S A FACT

Voyager 2 is the only spacecraft ever to fly by Uranus, passing by in 1989 — 12 years after launch.

The boys traveled deeper into space. "No wonder only one space probe has ever passed by Uranus," Jackson said. "This is really far out!"

It was getting late. The boys had only one more stop on their planet hop. Max couldn't wait to get home. He was getting hungry!

"Are we there yet?" Wyatt asked.

"Almost," Jackson said as he spotted another icy blue planet ahead. "Neptune is the eighth and final known planet in our solar system."

Suddenly, the spaceship rocked. It whooshed! It spun! "Neptune's winds!" Wyatt exclaimed. "They're more than one thousand miles per hour!"

The wind whipped the ship through space like a Frisbee!

IT'S A FACT

In 2006, New Horizons was launched to explore Pluto and the Kuiper belt beyond Neptune. In 2015, the satellite sent images and data of Pluto. Today, scientists are still receiving data from the edges of our solar system!

THUMP! The boys looked around. They were in their backyard, wishing on a shooting star.

"That was out of this world!" Wyatt exclaimed.

"Mission accomplished!" Jackson cheered. "But I'm spacing out! Time for bed!"

Max agreed with a loud crunch, as he watched his friends drift off to sleep.

Five Fast Facts

1. The four planets closest to the sun — Mercury, Venus, Earth, and Mars — are called the terrestrial planets because they have solid, rocky surfaces. Two of the outer planets — Jupiter and Saturn — are known as gas giants; the more distant Uranus and Neptune are called ice giants.

2. Our sun is a star. It is the closest star to Earth. That is why it appears larger than other stars we see.

3. Our solar system is located in the Milky Way galaxy. Scientists believe there are billions of other solar systems in our galaxy. And there are billions of galaxies in the **universe**.

4. The sun is the center of our solar system. Because it is so large it has a gravitational pull that holds the planets in its orbit. Without the sun, the planets would move out into dark outer space.

5. Thousands of asteroids, rocky worlds too small to be a planet, circle the sun in an asteroid belt between Mars and Jupiter.

New Discoveries

For 75 years, it was thought Pluto was a ninth planet in our solar system. Now scientists say Pluto is one of five or more dwarf planets. These are partly made of ice and are smaller than Earth's moon. Pluto and others are found in the Kuiper belt beyond Neptune and depend on Neptune's gravitational pull. Early in 2016, scientists in California said they had found evidence of a new Planet 9 with an egg-shaped orbit around our sun. It would be 10 times more massive than Earth and billions of miles beyond Pluto. It is so far away, it would take Planet 9 a mind-blowing 10,000 to 20,000 Earth-years to circle the sun!

Why is Earth the Only Planet with Life?

Take a deep breath! Earth is covered by a layer of air called atmosphere. Earth's air lets people, animals, and plants breathe. It also protects us from much of the sun's harmful rays. The atmosphere helps keep Earth at livable temperatures. As far as scientists know, Earth is also the only planet with lots of water (70% of Earth's surface). All living things need water to survive. All of this makes life on Earth possible.

Words to Keep

atmosphere: the gases surrounding Earth or other planets.

galaxy: millions or billions of stars held together by gravitational attraction and pull.

orbit: to travel completely around something; such as a spacecraft around a planet, or a planet's trip around the sun.

planet: a ball-shaped lump of rock, gas and metal that revolves around a star

universe: all existing matter and space, made up of endless numbers of galaxies

Learn More at the Library

Books

Aguilar, David A. *Space Encyclopedia: A Tour of Our Solar System and Beyond.* National Geographic Kids, 2013.

Higgins, Nadia. *The Solar System through Infographics.* Lerner Publications, 2014.

Simon, Seymour. *Our Solar System.* HarperCollins, revised edition, 2007.

Web Sites

National Aeronautics and Space Administration (NASA)
http://solarsystem.nasa.gov/kids/

European Space Agency
http://www.esa.int/esaKIDSen/index.html

Index